BASKETBALL LEGENDS

Kareem Abdul-Jabbar

Charles Barkley

Larry Bird

Wilt Chamberlain

Clyde Drexler

Julius Erving

Patrick Ewing

Anfernee Hardaway

Grant Hill

Magic Johnson

Michael Jordan

Jason Kidd

Reggie Miller

Hakeem Olajuwon

Shaquille O'Neal

Scottie Pippen

David Robinson

Dennis Rodman

CHELSEA HOUSE PUBLISHERS

BASKETBALL LEGENDS

JASON KIDD

Brant James

Introduction by
Chuck Daly

CHELSEA HOUSE PUBLISHERS
Philadelphia

Produced by Daniel Bial and Associates
New York, New York

Picture research by Alan Gottlieb
Cover illustration by Bradford Brown

First Printing

1 3 5 7 9 8 6 4 2

Library of Congress Cataloging-in-Publication Data

James, Brant.
        Jason Kidd/Brant James; Introduction by Chuck Daly.
            p. cm. -- (Basketball legends)
        Includes bibliographical reference and index.
        Summary: A biography of the talented point guard for the Dallas
        Mavericks who was named co-winner of the 1995 Rookie of the Year
        Award.
        ISBN 0-7910-4383-5 (alk. paper)
1. Kidd, Jason—Juvenile literature. 2. Basketball players—United States—
Biography—Juvenile literature. 3. Dallas Mavericks (Basketball team)—Juvenile literature. [1. Kidd, Jason. 2. Basketball players. 3. Racially mixed people—Biography.]
I. Title. II. Series.
GV884.K53J35   1997
796.323'092—dc21
[B]   96-53277
                                                             CIP
                                                             AC.

CONTENTS

BECOMING A BASKETBALL LEGEND

Chuck Daly

What does it take to be a basketball superstar? Two of the three things it takes are easy to spot. Any great athlete must have excellent skills and tremendous dedication. The third quality needed is much harder to define, or even put in words. Others call it leadership or desire to win, but I'm not sure that explains it fully. This third quality relates to the athlete's thinking process, a certain mentality and work ethic. One can coach athletic skills, and while few superstars need outside influence to help keep them dedicated, it is possible for a coach to offer some well-timed words in order to keep that athlete fully motivated. But a coach can do no more than appeal to a player's will to win; how much that player is then capable of ensuring victory is up to his own internal workings.

In recent times, we have been fortunate to have seen some of the best to play the game. Larry Bird, Magic Johnson, and Michael Jordan had all three components of superstardom in full measure. They brought their teams to numerous championships, and made the players around them better. (They also made their coaches look smart.)

I myself coached a player who belongs in that class, Isiah Thomas, who helped lead the Detroit Pistons to consecutive NBA crowns. Isiah is not tall-he's just over six feet-but he could do whatever he wanted with the ball. And what he wanted to do most was lead and win.

All the players I mentioned above and those whom this series will chronicle are tremendously gifted athletes, but for the most part, you can't play professional basketball at all unless you have excellent skills. And few players get to stay on their team unless they are willing to dedicate themselves to improving their talents even more, learning about their opponents, and finding a way to join with their teammates and win.

It's that third element that separates the good player from the superstar, the memorable players from the legends of the game. Superstars know when to take over the game. If the situation calls for a defensive stop, the superstars stand up and do it. If the situation calls for a key pass, they make it. And if the situation calls for a big shot, they want the ball. They don't want the ball simply because of their own glory or ego. Instead they know—and their teammates know—that they are the ones who can deliver, regardless of the pressure.

The words "legend" and "superstar" are often tossed around without real meaning. Taking a hard look at some of those who truly can be classified as "legends" can provide insight into the things that brought them to that level. All of them developed their legacy over numerous seasons of play, even if certain games will always stand out in the memories of those who saw them. Those games typically featured amazing feats of all-around play. No matter how great the fans thought the superstars were, these players were capable of surprising the fans, their opponents, and occasionally even themselves. The desire to win took over, and with their dedication and athletic skills already in place, they were capable of the most astonishing achievements.

CHUCK DALY, most recently the head coach of the New Jersey Nets, guided the Detroit Pistons to two straight NBA championships, in 1989 and 1990. He earned a gold medal as coach of the 1992 U.S. Olympic basketball team—the so-called "Dream Team"—and was inducted into the Pro Basketball Hall of Fame in 1994.

1
ON THE MAP

Jason Kidd had seen this all before, in super slow motion like the highlights of games he used to watch on television as a boy.

But this was not some Saturday afternoon TV show. Kidd wouldn't lace up his tennis shoes and take off into the street for a game against his school mates afterward. This was real. And now it was his turn to make the play and be the stuff of some other little kid's dreams.

Opponents knew they could not take him for granted. Kidd had already proved he was a complete player—able to shoot, pass, rebound, and run the offense. But he had never been in a really big college game before, whereas most of his opponents had. His opponents were just waiting for him to crack.

One minute, 11 seconds remained on the clock in the second round of the 1993 National Collegiate Athletic Association men's basketball tour-

Jason Kidd's explosive first step takes him past Duke's Bobby Hurley in the 1993 NCAA Midwest regional second-round game.

nament. This was March Madness, the big dance, and the score was tied, 77-77.

Kidd dribbled, dribbled, dribbled at the top of the key in the gold and blue of the California Golden Bears, looking for a crack in the defense. The 19-year-old basketball prodigy was already a household name in northern California and millions of other Americans, watching on live television, would soon know his name as well.

They watched every dribble. And they watched his nemesis, college basketball's current best and most-revered point guard, Duke University's Bobby Hurley, shadowing his every move.

Crowning moments are achieved by overcoming great obstacles, and the mountain at this moment was high: Cal was pitted against the Duke Blue Devils, the two-time defending champion team of college basketball.

Duke had steamrollered mediocre teams and top teams alike. Besides Bobby Hurley, other team greats were forward Grant Hill, center Cherokee Parks, and coach Mike Krzyzewski. Duke had gone to the Final Four (the semi-finals) four years in a row, and here Cal had to face them in just the second round of play. The Blue Devils were used to celebrating as the clock ran out.

Dribble, dribble. Now.

Kidd sprung. He burst forward, then drove to left baseline until a defender's body suddenly blocked his way. In the far right corner he spotted teammate Lamond Murray spotting up.

Kidd whizzed a pass toward his wide-open teammate, but Hurley, battle-hardened from four seasons of Atlantic Coast Conference and NCAA tournament wars, sensed the freshman's intent and deflected it into a hive of scrambling players in the lane.

Kidd swooped under the basket and snatched up the ball. With one quick step he was airborne. Bodies clad in white and bodies in blue went up with him.

It was time to create. Kidd tossed the ball out into the air with his right hand and took an opponent's forearm across his. Still, the ball sailed true. It tumbled through the basket to the screech of an official's whistle and the roar of an arena full of people.

Cal led, 79-77, and Kidd strode to the free-throw line and swished the penalty shot to give the Golden Bears a three-point lead.

Kidd celebrates Cal's upset of two-time defending champion Duke University along with teammate Alfred Grigsby.

Duke was hardly finished. Hurley fired a three-point bomb in an attempt to the tie the game. But the senior, who had played every minute of the game, saw his shot clang off the rim; his weary arms were unable to find his customary stroke.

Murray grabbed the rebound and was fouled. He hit both shots and an 82-77 upset was sealed.

Cal celebrated its biggest basketball win in decades. And a star was born: Jason Kidd, basketball's next big star.

2

FULLBACK WITH A BASKETBALL

Frank Laporte knew he was dealing with something special from the first time he saw Jason Kidd. The head boys' basketball coach and athletic director at St. Joseph's of Notre Dame in Alameda, CA, was not allowed by rules to recruit the eighth-grader, but he knew the talented kid by reputation.

Laporte had never met Kidd, but he had heard Jason was interested in playing for St. Joseph's, and after watching a St. Joseph's grammar school team play in 1987, he had this fact confirmed.

"I was walking outside and all of a sudden somebody yelled at me," Laporte recalls. "It was Jason. He said he was going to be playing for me next year."

Kidd's prep school career began in earnest that summer when he immediately began impressing Laporte in a summer varsity league. Kidd,

---

Even as a high school student, Kidd's talent made him one of the best known athletes in the San Francisco area.

not even yet a freshman, was already leaps and bounds ahead of his upperclassmen teammates, and wrested a spot on the varsity for himself that fall. Only Calvin Bird, St. Joseph's senior center, who later played at Villanova University, was further developed than Kidd.

For Laporte, the decision to place the freshman on varsity was not a tough one. "I know a lot of coaches don't like to put a freshman on varsity, but I've never had a real policy against it," he said. "If they can handle it, I let them play. If I had kept Jason Kidd on junior varsity he would not have been challenged. That would have been a wasted year for him."

Scrutiny became Kidd's companion from an early age; not because of what he did, but what he was. Jason's father, Steve, a now-retired TWA supervisor, is black, and his mother, Anne, a former bank bookkeeper, is white. In a society where such things unfortunately still matter to some, Jason—along with his two sisters—was instantly different. His parents, though, helped assure that his background made him *special*, not different. Family is still a major part of Kidd's life today. His father traveled to all but two of his college games.

"I had two different cultures and two different backgrounds to learn from," Kidd said in an article in *The Sporting News*.

Kidd's talent began to shine through as early as fourth grade when the little tornado scored 21 of his team's 30 points in a Catholic-league basketball game.

Kidd, an avid lover of the then-and-now-Oakland Raiders, displayed his athleticism and his "Just win, baby" attitude at the expense of a mailbox during a Thanksgiving football game his sixth-grade year. Kidd caught a pass, plowed over a mailbox, and kept going. To this day, coaches describe him as "a fullback with a basketball."

Kidd enjoyed many sports besides basketball. Although he crashed over a mailbox while scoring a touchdown in that Thanksgiving game of backyard football, his parents got him to give up the game. Instead, he had become a gifted soccer and baseball player by his teen years. It was rumored early in 1996 that Kidd had expressed an interest in playing minor league baseball like NBA legend Michael Jordan had attempted two years earlier.

In high school, Kidd hit .333 with a .500 on-base percentage his senior season for a team that finished 27-5. The centerfielder hit three home runs and collected 20 RBIs that season. He considered playing baseball in college after his freshman season.

Kidd did not enter prep school a completely finished basketball player despite his many skills. He was a scorer but not a shooter, and Laporte spent much time attempting to correct Kidd's jumpshot, which did not have a high arc. He dubbed the shot a "frozen rope" and explained to Kidd that arcing the ball gave him a greater chance of sinking the attempt than just shooting in a straight line.

Kidd compensated for his streaky outside touch by slashing to the basket for layups or penetrating and whizzing the ball to open teammates as the defense collapsed. Suddenly everyone around Kidd was improving also.

St. Joseph's flourished during Kidd's freshman campaign as the wily point guard dished out 263 assists, scored 376 points, grabbed 278 rebounds, and made 157 steals.

Kidd was named "California State Frosh Player of the Year," made the "All-Northern California Team" and the "All-East Bay" first team, and was an "All-Alameda County" first-teamer for his efforts. It was during that season that former UNLV head coach Jerry Tarkanian called him "the next Magic Johnson."

Kidd stepped up his leadership role and his game performances immeasurably his sophomore season, doling out 320 assists, scoring 645 points, snaring 297 rebounds, and making 168 steals.

"Jason's first year he kind of sat back," Laporte said. "He did the same thing at Cal. But his second year, when Calvin was gone, he took over the leadership aspect."

Kidd added more hardware to his trophy case after his sophomore season, being named East Shore Athletic League, Oakland, California, South County, and East Bay "player of the year" and being named to the state first team.

By his junior year, Kidd mania had begun to boil over. College offers came in droves, and the demand to see the Pilots' star was so great that St. Joseph's home games often had to be moved out of its small gym to the Oakland Coliseum, home of the NBA's Golden State Warriors. One game, against St. Joseph's chief rival, Bishop O'Dowd, drew 11,000 fans at the Coliseum. Kidd seemed to come up with his best efforts in the big games. In one meeting against Bishop O'Dowd, he scored all 22 St. Joseph's points in the fourth quarter.

The St. Joseph's athletic department, which sponsors 11 sports, soon began reaping the benefits of its marquee player. The school began marketing a complete line of Jason Kidd sports-

Kidd leads the parade celebrating St. Joseph's victory in the state basketball championships.

wear. Almost anything, seemingly, could be purchased with the prep star's image: hats, T-shirts, sweatshirts, and posters. Kidd was well on his way to becoming as recognizable a figure in the Bay Area as San Francisco 49ers quarterback Joe Montana.

St. Joseph's once financed a cross-country trip to a basketball tournament by auctioning off 250 balls that Kidd had autographed.

Kidd helped fire the growing excitement his junior and senior years by leading the Pilots to the Division 1 state championship over schools with at least three times St. Joseph's enrollment. California schools are bracketed for state tournament play by number of students, with Division 1 being the biggest at 1,500-3,000 students. Even though St. Joseph's has fewer than 500 students, Laporte likes his team to play in a division higher than the one for which they qualify.

Kidd dished out 237 assists his junior season, scored 754 points, grabbed 309 rebounds, and managed 145 steals to help the Pilots march to a state title over Freemont (Los Angeles).

National recognition began to pour in atop his California laurels as he was named All-American by two of the nation's most-respected prep/college basketball magazines: *Street and Smith*, and *Parade.*

The Pilots cruised to another state title his senior year with the help of a 21-point effort from Kidd in the championship game. It was the senior's defense that won Laporte's favor that day, however. "The other team only had four points midway through the second period," he remembers. "What a defender! It was like Kidd had eyes in the back of his head."

Kidd posted career highs in points (886), assists (345), and steals (249) his final prep season. He only grabbed 258 rebounds, however, a career low, as he had more help in that department from his teammates.

In four years, Kidd had 719 steals and 2,661 points, both school records. His 1,155 career assists set a state record. A 46-point single-game effort also set a school record, and he shot 54 percent from the field, 82 percent from the foul line, and 36 percent from three-point range.

Few basketball players get to score a triple double—reaching double figures in three different box-score categories—but in high school, Kidd almost added a quadruple-double to his resume. At the Beach Ball Classic, an annual

Kidd held a news conference to announce that he would attend the University of California. With him were his mother and father and Coach Laporte (left).

showcase of some of the nation's best teams held in Myrtle Beach, South Carolina, St. Joseph was paired in a consolation game against St. Raymond's. Kidd produced 38 points, 13 rebounds, 10 steals, and 9 assists. He had a legitimate chance at getting one more assist in the last minutes when he pumped the ball inside to a teammate, who, assumedly unaware of the importance of him scoring, fed the ball outside to another player.

"He did everything but sell peanuts that day," Laporte chuckled.

Kidd again won his host of regional awards, including a new one—"Pacific Region Player of the Year"—and *Parade* named him its national co-player of the year. *USA Today* tabbed him as national "player of the year."

Kidd finished his prep career with an average of 20.3 points per game, 8.82 assists, 8.68 rebounds, and 5.49 steals, an amazing set of all-around numbers from a point guard. Even more amazing for a point guard was the fact he finished his career as the number six all-time prep scorer in California history.

Local media put his name above those of two former Bay Area prep stars, Bill Russell and Bill Cartwright, both professional basketball legends.

St. Joseph's was an astounding 122-14 during Kidd's reign, and two of the losses came during his freshman season when he was suspended for missing a curfew.

Kidd still loves to appear each year at St. Joseph's summer basketball camp to lend a little hands-on advice. "He's just great with the kids," Laporte says. "It's obvious he likes working with them, and he'll sign anything. This one kid once didn't have anything for him to sign, so we went and grabbed a Coke can he had just finished with. And Jason signed it."

By the spring of Kidd's senior year, acres of forest had given itself up for the pounds of recruiting letters he received, and the school's phone lines were hot with calls from anxious scouts around the nation. Tiny little St. Joseph's of Notre Dame had become the recruiting center of the universe.

Kidd began spending his lunch periods in Laporte's office, chatting about his future, and eliminating the middle man when the phone rang. "It was always for him anyway," Laporte said. "I'd just put him right on the line."

The Universities of Arizona, Kentucky, Kansas, and Ohio State all were very interested. Only Othella Harrington—who chose to attend Georgetown—got nearly as much recruiting attention that year.

Golden State Warriors head coach Don Nelson suggested the point guard could skip college completely and vault directly into the NBA. Nelson insisted Kidd could have been drafted no lower than the second round, and would have played immediately.

Kidd seemed to validate this point when he was named most valuable player of a summer pro-am league in San Francisco the summer after his senior year in high school

When he chose to attend Cal, San Franciscans rejoiced while fans at the other schools cried in their beer.

3
GOLDEN BEAR

Part of Kidd's decision to stay close to home stemmed from finding comfort in familiarity. He wanted, he said, to stay near his family and friends. And he was already acquainted with Cal and its players, most notably Monty Buckley, who became a close friend. Kidd routinely frequented Cal's gym as a prep, playing pickup games with Golden Bears players, enjoying working with players whose skill levels were closer to his than those he found in high school.

A large force was provided by his parents, who wanted him close, and who apparently very much liked then-Cal head coach Lou Campanelli's academic standards for players. When Kidd's parents met with Campanelli, they liked the fact that he talked more about passing grades than passing basketballs.

Kidd had been able to enjoy a relatively sane life in the immediate months following St.

Coach Todd Bozeman has a word with his star point guard as the Golden Bears go through a workout at Harmon gym.

23

Expectations were high on December 1, 1992, as Kidd was introduced at his first collegiate basketball game.

Joseph's charge to a second state title. But how could he relax when major area newspapers were counting the days to his debut and speculating about how good the team might be?

In the late 1950s, the University of California won a national championship over Jerry West and the West Virginia Mountaineers. But for the next 30 years, Cal was known for its scholars, not dribblers. They year before Kidd arrived, the basketball team compiled a 10-18 record.

But fans clamored with excitement—and for tickets to Golden Bears games—once it was known he was coming to campus. Cal games had sold out in many of the previous years, but the hordes of no-shows at each contest provided less than a fearsome home-court feel.

Cal's season-opening practice, "Night Court," what most schools dub "midnight madness," was packed by nearly 5,000 fans in Kidd's freshman season. Previous seasons' opening practices had been sparsely populated, but the new era of optimism sparked by Kidd's prediction that he would lead the Bears to the NCAA Tournament's Final Four in two seasons took hold.

Cal, which marketed the entire season around Kidd's arrival, moved five home games before the season even started from its 6,578-seat on-campus Harmon Arena to the 15,000-capacity Oakland Coliseum. Cal had received more than 500 ticket inquiries the day Kidd announced he would attend Berkeley.

The Golden Bears were clearly a better team with Kidd on it. But halfway through that first year, Campanelli was fired and Kidd found himself at the center of the controversy. University officials claimed the head coach was demoralizing the team. An article in the *San Francisco Examiner* quoted a Cal official as saying Steve Kidd had alleged Campanelli was putting so much pressure on his son it was making him "physically ill." Steve Kidd denied the charge.

The man who recruited Kidd, assistant coach Todd Bozeman, assumed the head coaching chores February 12. At age 29, he was one of the nation's youngest Division I coaches.

Neither Kidd nor Cal missed a beat, and they actually improved, finishing 9-1 to take a head of steam into Cal's just second NCAA tourney in the last 33 years.

Kidd became the fifth freshman in Pac-10 history to be named to the all-conference team. He averaged 13 points, 7.7 assists, 4.9 rebounds, and 3.8 steals per game his freshman year. His steal effort—boosted by a Cal-record 8 in a game against Washington—set an NCAA freshman record. His 110 total thefts broke the Pac-10 standard set by Gary Payton, a former high school and future NBA rival of Kidd, and his per-game average established a new NCAA freshman mark. He also was one of only two players in the nation to be in the top ten in both steals and assists, all of which helped seal his selection as Freshman of the Year by *The Sporting News* and *USA Today*.

He proved he was a scorer with a 27-point effort against perennial Pac-10 power Arizona midway through his first season, and he added 25 more three games later against USC.

But Kidd was not concerned with how his box-score line read. His all-out hustle, his court-presence, lifted his teammates. "Jason's not just a statistical player," teammate Ryan Jamison said. "He might get big numbers, but that still doesn't tell you what he does for the team. If he gets two steals in a game, that's as good as making the point guard think twice about every pass he throws."

Golden Bears players knew Kidd could deliver the ball for an assist from any angle. If they wanted to score, though, they'd need to stay alert. A moment of inattention and a bullet pass from Kidd could send the ball bouncing off their foreheads.

Cal began NCAA tournament play amidst a wave of hoopla. Cal had been a stranger to the tourney for a long time, and the kid had brought them back. His pre-season predictions of a Final Four march made Cal, even for casual observers, a team to watch.

Cal opened the tourney against the Louisiana State University squad, and Kidd was finally provided with a live nation-wide forum for his amazing collection of skills. LSU no longer had Shaquille O'Neal on its crew, but Coach Dale Brown always put out a well-honed team on the floor.

Cal led, 36-29, at halftime. The Tigers fought back to tie the game, 64-64, in a game that was suddenly becoming frenetic. LSU's Andre Owen barely missed a three-point shot and a chance for a lead that Cal rebounded, giving the ball to Kidd for one last possession with 22 seconds left.

The 17,463 fans at the Rosemont Horizon stiffened in anticipation as the Bears set up in a spread offense, Kidd's teammates sprinkled along the baseline, he at the top of the key pounding a rhythmic dribble.

Kidd watched the clock slowly slip down inside 10 seconds. Then he sliced quickly past his defender with a dribble, knifed through the lane, and briefly whirled his back to the gathering Tiger defense. Kidd then skipped between forward Lenear Burns and 7'0" center Geert Hammink and accelerated into the air as he approached the hoop. He drew the ball below his waist as he soared, then brought it toward

Jason Kidd eyes the loose ball and the fast-break opportunities as he gets away from the big paw of LSU's Geert Hammink in the first round of the 1993 NCAA tournament. LSU's Clarence Ceasar is at right.

his chest and released a scoop shot as the final seconds ticked away.

The shot arced above the rim, then plunged through the net as the final tick fell off the clock. Cal 66, LSU 64.

Brown, who would not shake Bozeman's hand after the game, possibly as a negative reaction as many coaches had to Campanelli's ouster, was amazed by Kidd's last-second effort. "I don't know how he did it," Brown said. "It was the kind of shot we would have wanted him to take."

Hammink, in a keen assessment, coined a phrase that resounded throughout the tourney. "He earned it the pretzel way," he said.

Murray led Cal with 23 points, and Kidd chipped in 7 assists and 16 points.

Both Cal and Kidd faced a monstrous challenge in the second round of the tournament. Two-time defending national champion Duke, which the season before had stunned Jerry Tarkanian's UNLV to win the title, stood in the Bears' path to the Sweet 16. Blue Devils players were household names—Grant Hill, Thomas Hill, Cherokee Parks, and their wily point guard, the hard-nosed senior Bobby Hurley, the NCAA's all-time assist leader, who had taken his team to the Final Four three times.

Kidd won his personal battle, wearing down the dogged Hurley, and helped Cal win the war with 14 assists, 11 points, 8 rebounds, and 4 steals in the 82-77 upset that set the nation abuzz.

Cal began the game with a flourish when Kidd hit Murray with an alley-oop pass for a slam dunk, and led, 47-37, at halftime as the Blue Devils committed 12 first-half turnovers, thanks, in part, to Kidd's defense pressure, and a poor

37-percent shooting effort. Cal eventually out-shot Duke 50 percent to 38 percent.

Time after time Hill and Parks came up just short on shots, and the inspired Golden Bears were ready to push the other way.

Duke at times had no offense except for Hurley, who eventually pumped in 32 points to keep his team alive for one final, desperate push.

A severe ankle injury to Parks just before half-time limited the Blue Devils even further, and Cal responded with a 23-6 run over the last four minutes of the first half and first two of the second half to lead by 18 points. But, like the champions they were, Duke rallied to pare the lead and actually led, 77-76, with 2:21 left when Thomas Hill hit a foul shot.

"I expected Duke to make that kind of comeback effort," Bozeman said. "They were, after all, the defending national champions. You know they will rise."

Kidd's impatience had allowed the Blue Devils back in, but his talent would not let them steal his day. With 1:11 left Kidd hit his amazing shot in the paint, and Cal rallied behind that determined effort to stave off Duke. Kidd hit one of two free throws with 38 seconds left for an 80-77 lead, and Murray snagged a super-important rebound on Duke's next possession when Hurley missed a three-point try. Murray then salted the game away with foul shots.

The win was sweet for Cal not only because it had come over the defending national champs, but because it had defended the honor and spirit of the team and the head coach.

After the LSU game, Brown had been asked what Cal's prospects against Duke were. "I don't

Kidd not only could run the offense as well as any guard in college, he was also known for his ferocious defense.

think they have a prayer," he answered. Kidd repeated those words in the Horizon lockerroom before the Golden Bears took the floor against Duke.

Kidd finished with 14 assists and 11 points. Murray led the Bears with 28 points, and Jerod Haase added 13 more.

Cal's miracle ride ended soon after, however, perhaps because it mentally exhausted itself in the Duke upset, perhaps because it finally met a better team. But the University of Kansas bounced the Golden Bears from the tourney with a 93-76 shellacking, and Kidd's promise to no-look-pass them into the Final Four had been left unfulfilled.

A killer 22-6 Jayhawks run doomed Cal midway through the second half. The Golden Bears had actually led, 52-48, in the second half, but the monster run gave Kansas a 70-58 bulge with just 7:08 left.

Ironically, it was Kansas' outstanding guard tandem that powered both the run and the Jayhawks' victory. One of those players would not have even been on the floor had Kidd accepted head coach Roy Williams' invitation to Lawrence. But, then again, Cal probably would not have been there without Kidd.

Williams, who had recruited Kidd heavily out of St. Joseph's of Notre Dame, was obviously as impressed with him after seeing him play intercollegiately as when he saw him as a Bay Area prep star. The Jayhawks mentor called Kidd one of the top three point guard prospects he had ever seen in 15 years of college coaching. The others? Kenny Anderson of Georgia Tech and Derek Harper of Illinois—both of whom became All-Stars in the NBA.

For all he had proved over the past half year, Kidd was not impressed with himself. "I had an average season," he told reporters. "I have a lot to work on."

Much of the improvement needed to come in the shooting department, the only area for which Kidd was chided. He shot 46.3 percent from the field during the regular season (28.5 percent on three-pointers), and just 65.7 percent from the free-throw line.

Teams want the ball in the point guard's hands in crunchtime, especially if the point guard is Kidd, but that poor effort from the foul line made him an easy choice to foul.

Improving that jumper meant more to Kidd than just pumping up his scoring totals. "I know I have to make that pull-up jump shot from the free-throw line or the three-pointer off the fast-break or people are going to play off me," he said.

During that summer, Kidd played on Team USA, a traveling squad of American collegians that toured Europe facing other national teams. He averaged 8.4 points, 4.2 rebounds, and 4.0 assists per game on the five-date tour. He also enjoyed informal workouts with Michigan's Jalen Rose and Gary Payton of the Seattle Super-Sonics.

For the start of Kidd's sophomore season, basketball pundits ranked the Golden Bears sixth in the nation. A newly imposed 35-second shot clock was sure to make the game more of a run-and-gun affair on all nights, and the prospect of a full season under Bozeman's aggressive offense suited Kidd just fine.

With notoriety came more scrutiny, as usual, and Kidd tried to grow a beard to keep people from so quickly recognizing him as he strode through Sather Gate, headphones over ears. (It didn't work.) The hysteria grew to such a pitch that during the season security guards had to escort the team to and from the lockerroom. On one occasion at a game at the University of Washington, two fans hid in his locker and jumped out when the team entered the lockerroom.

Kidd welcomed the new season with 27 points against Santa Clara and continued to improve each night. He set a Cal and Pac-10 record with 18 assists against archrival Stanford, and produced 18 points, 14 rebounds, and 12 assists in a shocking upset of top-ranked UCLA on January 29, 1994. That triple-double was one of four for Kidd his sophomore year. Kidd scored 17 points with 11 rebounds and 11 assists against Maryland-Baltimore County, posted the exact same numbers against Arizona, and scored 15 points with 10 rebounds, and 18 assists against Stanford. Most college players—including Michael Jordan, Isaiah Thomas, Danny Manning, Chris Webber, and Juwan Howard—went their entire careers without creating one triple-double.

Kidd finished his sophomore season with an average of 16.7 points, an astounding 9.1 assists (which led the nation), 6.9 rebounds, and 3.1 steals per game. Kidd was fourth nationally in steals.

Kidd's effort's earned him first-team All-America honors from *The Associated Press* with Duke's Hill, Connecticut's Donyell Marshall, Purdue's Glenn Robinson, and Louisville's Clifford Rozier. He was the first Cal player to be named to the team since 1968. Kidd, who led the Pac-10 in both assists and steals (and set the conference single-season record with 272), and who set the school career theft record (204) in just two seasons, was also named conference player of the year. He was the first Golden Bear and first sophomore ever bestowed with that honor.

Cal's upset of the Bruins propelled them to a second-place tie in the Pac-10 at 13-5. Cal boasted a better record overall, however, at 22-8. UCLA finished 21-7. Arizona won the regular-season conference race at 14-4.

Cal's finish earned it a fifth seed in the West Region of the NCAA tourney, which meant it did not have to endure a tremendously long trip for its first-round play.

Speculation had begun in pre-season that this tournament would be Kidd's last. Most scouts and observers felt he had little else to gain from any more intercollegiate play. Kidd himself remained non-committal as he tried to concentrate on his season, but the nagging uncertainty remained. As he entered his second NCAA tourney his promise rang clear in both a confident and cryptic way: Cal, Final Four, two years.

Two years. And then time's up?

Kidd proved to be a poor prognosticator. In their first game, Cal faced, unranked, unher-

Kidd makes a leaping pass in the Bears' final home game at the Oakland Coliseum. Cal beat the Oregon State Beavers in the 1994 game.

alded, and undaunted Wisconsin-Green Bay, a small school located across the street from the Green Bay Packers' offices. The game was played relatively close to Cal's home, in Ogden, Utah.

Kidd was sorry to leave college before graduating. But he did not mind all the attention his announcement drew.

The Phoenix were led by sophomore center Jeff Nordgaard (15.3 points per game) and on paper could not match the Golden Bears' fastbreak or half-court potential. Wisconsin-GB, making just its second trip ever to the NCAA tourney, would need a nearly perfect game to beat Cal.

Nordgaard and The Phoenix delivered, providing the upset of the first round in a 61-57 stunner. Cal was woeful from the field, hitting just 34 percent of its shots and self-destructing in crucial situations all game. Open shot after open shot clanged off the back iron or rimmed out, and the persistent and disciplined Phoenix allowed little margin for error.

Nordgaard helped stage the upset with 9 rebounds and a game-high 24 points and stymied a Golden Bears run in the final minute with the score tied, 57-57. Nordgaard broke open along the baseline and splashed a 12-footer for a 59-57 advantage and forced the Bears into hurry-up mode.

Kidd drove down the center of the court with 15.2 seconds left and fired a potential game-tying shot. Unlike the heroic shots he had taken against Duke and LSU, this one did not fall. Wisconsin-GB grabbed the rebound and secured the win with foul shots.

Kidd shot a miserable 4 for 17 from the field, and missed the crucial last-ditch shot Cal desperately needed. Although he pulled down 11 rebounds, he also committed five turnovers in the second half. "Whenever we made a run I'd throw the ball away," he told reporters after the game. "I take the blame for this because I believe it was my fault."

Kidd had said before his sophomore season that he might be inclined to stay in college if the Golden Bears did not reach the 1993-94 Final Four. And, he said, if he stayed for the junior year, leaving before his senior year would be dumb because he would be "so close to graduating."

Those words came as prayers of hope for Cal fans, but it was clear Kidd had nothing left to prove at Berkeley. A rumored rookie salary cap, which eventually did go in effect the next season, also helped him reach a decision.

Almost 200 people jammed into the Hall of Fame Room in Cal's Memorial Stadium, March 23, 1994, the day of Kidd's 21st birthday, to hear Kidd announce he was making himself available for the NBA draft. One fan tried unsuccessfully to buy tickets to the event. Another was arrested for masquerading as a reporter and refusing to leave. A policeman ticketed Kidd's truck outside the building, then hung around until after the press conference to have Kidd autograph it.

Coach Bozeman looked on philosophically. "The sad part," he said, "is it's like being happy and sad because it's like your younger brother moving on."

4

GOOD DRAFTS
AND BAD

The early summer of 1994 should have been the most wondrous time of Jason Kidd's life. He had just finished an amazingly successful college career, and his rising stock in the upcoming NBA draft in June nearly guaranteed him a selection as a high lottery pick, meaning an equally high salary and financial security for him and his family for the rest of their lives.

The talented, charismatic 21-year-old seemingly had the world in his hands as firmly and as surely as a basketball. But there were tempestuous times ahead.

Just 30 days before the draft, Kidd was driving a Toyota Landrover he had bought for his father. It was late at night and Kidd was motoring on a freeway near his home; in the car were two companions and a woman named Alexan-

The Dallas Mavericks were an immediately improved team once Jason Kidd joined their ranks. Here he shoots a layup ahead of Olden Polynice of the Sacramento Kings as the Mavs went on to win by two points.

37

dria Brown. Suddenly, Kidd lost control of the car. It flipped, hit a wall, and skidded 150 yards before coming to a stop.

Kidd admits that what he did next was stupid and all his fault. He and Alexandria Brown fled the scene, leaving the others at the crash site.

Kidd was not injured physically, but his reputation was nearly ruined. It later came out that Kidd may have been driving in excess of 110 miles per hour when the car crashed. Kidd pled no contest to charges of speeding and was sentenced to two years probation, 100 hours of community service, and fined the maximum, $1,000.

It also turned out that Alexandria Brown was the mother of Kidd's child. Kidd had never lived with Brown, then 21, and had originally contested that he was the father of the child later born Jason Alexander Kidd. A blood test proved Kidd was the father, and after months of legal wrangling, courts arranged for Kidd to fulfill his responsibility and pay child support. News of the paternity suit was splashed across San Francisco and Oakland newspapers the day of the NBA draft.

Then Kidd was sued for $250,000 on June 17 for allegedly smacking a female friend of a friend at his 21st birthday party March 23, the day he announced he was leaving Cal to enter the draft. The Alameda County District Attorney's Office said there was not enough evidence, however, to pursue the suit, and dropped the case. Kidd claimed it was a case of "money grubbing," someone trying to cash in quickly on his fame and impending fortune.

Whatever the circumstances, and whatever the result, that late spring and early summer proved that Kidd was a lightning rod for infamy as much as fame. Would these recent events change his basketball career? When a professional team signs a player, it not only wants to know about his jump shot, it wants to know about his character. Does he take drugs? Is he in trouble with the law? Does he have good work habits? Before a team bestows a million-dollar contract, it wants to know that the player will be able to live up to his potential—on and off the court.

With the Milwaukee Bucks, owners of the top pick in the draft, all but certain to select Purdue's Glenn "Big Dog" Robinson—the 1994 College Player of the Year—frenzied discussion had begun about whether Kidd was a safe pick at number two for the Dallas Mavericks. Basketball analysts such as ESPN's Dick Vitale began suggesting Kidd's troubles had become too much of a risk for the Mavericks, a sad-sack franchise with a history of bad luck and a worse drafting record.

Suddenly Grant Hill, Duke's dynamic small forward with the squeaky-clean image, became a media darling and a favorite for the second pick. "The Mavericks will take Grant Hill," Vitale said before the draft, "because [Mavs owner] Don Carter likes him and Kidd would be another blunder."

From a sure-fire number two pick to a blunder? Kidd's stock was falling in the media amidst reports Mavericks head coach Dick Motta was unimpressed the one time he saw Kidd in person—in his final intercollegiate game, the loss to Wisconsin-Green Bay—and did not like giving rookies the huge responsibility of running point.

And so came draft day, and after the Bucks presented Robinson with one of their gaudy new purple-and-green jerseys, Dallas was on the clock.

Don Leventhal, who has scouted college basketball players since 1985 and publishes *The Don Leventhal NBA Draft Report,* gushed over Kidd in a pre-draft analysis:

"[Kidd] is extremely fundamentally sound, has superior court awareness and is one of the rare players who truly has the ability to make his teammates better. Tremendous passer and defender who plays the game with intensity. Good speed, great quickness, and moves well without the ball. Is a better shooter than he is given credit for and will likely get better."

Could the Mavericks pass this up? No. It turns out they never even spoke with Grant Hill. Kidd was their expected choice all the way.

And maybe the selection was in part governed by fate. For years Kidd had left a Mavericks hat in the back of his mother's car. Why? For some reason he thought he might play for them one day, and besides, he said, green is his favorite color.

The Dallas Mavericks needed Jason Kidd maybe as much as he needed them. In existence since 1980, the franchise had struggled to carve a niche for itself in a city that loved football, especially the Dallas Cowboys. The blue-and-green squad had done little in recent years to carve that niche, at times making its home, Reunion Arena, a house of pain.

A lot of the Mavs' problems stemmed from poor or unlucky drafting. Dallas's first draft pick ever, UCLA's Kiki Vandeweghe, never played a game for the club. And with few exceptions—two luckily just before Kidd's arrival—the Mavs' first-round harvest, where teams' futures are made, was a rotten crop.

Dallas enjoyed its best season in 1986-87 when the team won the Midwest Division. They created that squad by good drafts in 1981 and 1983. They had the first pick in 1981 and used it on DePaul's Mark Aguirre; they also got Kansas State's Rolando Blackmon at number nine. In 1983, they took Tennessee's Dale Ellis at number nine, and Illinois' Derek Harper at 11. In 1982, however, they suffered a bust in Wyoming's Bill Garnett. Dallas had another draft hit in Sam Perkins of North Carolina, whom they picked at number 15 in 1984. The next year, Dallas possessed three first-round picks. Two players (Washington's Detlef Schrempf at number eight and St. John's Bill Wennington at 16) went on to forge solid NBA careers—but not with the Mavericks. The other, Indiana's Uwe Blab at number 17, averaged 2.2 points and 1.6 rebounds in four seasons in Dallas before being dropped from the team in 1989.

Dallas entered its deepest depths from 1986 to 1991, taking Michigan's Roy Tarpley, whose career was marred countless times by recurrent drug problems, Alabama's Jim Farmer (waived the next season after averaging 2.0 points and 5.2 minutes per game), Louisiana Tech's Randy White (maybe taking a Cowboys namesake was a marketing ploy), and Missouri's Doug Smith. White was a bit player for five seasons and Smith was left unprotected and taken by the Toronto Raptors in the June, 1995 expansion draft.

The last time the Mavs made the playoffs was in 1990. Their 22-60 in 1991-92 at least let them

Kidd worked hard in practice to develop the stamina the long NBA season requires.

On the day Kidd learned he would start in the 1995 All-Star game, he celebrated with a dunk over Golden State's Keith Jennings.

draft Ohio State guard Jim Jackson and their 11-71 record in 1992-3 was only brightened by the right to select Kentucky's Jamal Mashburn. Jackson provided Dallas with a sharp shooting guard, and Mashburn is a flashy small forward.

But more importantly, it gave them two building blocks. Two Js.

Kidd gave them the distributor, The Three Js, and basketball in Dallas was starting to look like something fun again.

But sunshine and moonbeams were not in order quite yet. Kidd failed to report for a mid-summer workout camp geared expressly for rookies to become acclimated to the team's workings before pre-season camp began in the fall. Kidd said he did not want to risk an injury before his contract was finalized—even though the Mavericks offered him a $36-million insurance policy for the four-day camp. This came as an unsettling signal from a player who had told Motta on draft day he would "crawl" there if he had to.

The Mavericks should have been used to such trouble. Jackson had held out of the same 1992-93 mini-camp and nearly forced a trade before the season started because of a long contract dispute. Friction rapidly developed between Mashburn and then-head coach Quinn Buckner, himself a former star player. Mashburn's season-long feud with Buckner was no secret throughout the 1993-94 campaign, one where the Mavericks answered their 11-71 season with a 13-69 follow-up. Average home attendance fell to 12,839, the lowest since the Mavs' third season, and Buckner was fired at season's end, partly, rumors circulated, because of the Mashburn situation. Buckner was fired May 3, 1994. Mashburn signed an eight-year contract with Dallas five months later.

Motta, the Mavs' first coach, who had retired May 20, 1987, had been rehired almost seven years later to the day to sort out the mess. But with Kidd a no-show and no contract-signing in sight, things looked like business—bad business—as usual in Dallas.

That all changed September 2 when Kidd signed a nine-year deal worth more than $54 million, with up to $60 million in incentives, not even counting his $800,000 endorsement contract with Nike.

All in all, Kidd's eventual signing put him in a more positive light. He put pen to paper before top-pick Robinson and third-pick Hill, meaning he chose not to use any huge contracts they might have garnered as leverage. The contract still was the largest in Dallas sports history.

Kidd's ensuing comments also seemed to assuage worries about his personality. "It takes a lot for a young person like me to step forward to be one of the first to sign, to not worry about whether other people are going to talk about it," he said. "But I was dedicated to signing early because I wanted to get in and learn from (assistant) Coach (Brad) Davis and Coach Motta as early as I can."

Basketball fans were suddenly breathing a little easier in Dallas. The monster Jason Kidd they had

Jimmy Jackson is a multi-talented but inconsistent player. Jason Kidd stirred up difficulties when he said he did not want to play with Jackson.

been anticipating was suddenly turning into a model citizen who followed his signing by donating $50,000 to an area community center. All the right public relations moves were being made, or maybe the genuine Kidd was showing himself.

Kidd's NBA coming-out party was held November 5, 1994, in a Reunion Arena packed with a sellout crowd of 17,502. The rookie did not disappoint, showing his new peers and Mavericks fans that once on-court, he was the master of his surroundings. Kidd scored 10 points, dealt out 10 assists, and grabbed 9 rebounds and 3 steals as the Mavs downed the New Jersey Nets, 112-103, for the franchise's first season-opening win in seven years.

Kidd pumped up his scoring and pumped Dallas to 2-1 (just 11 wins shy of the 1993-94 win-total after just six days) by scoring 19 points with 9 rebounds and 5 assists in a road-opening 107-100 win over the Philadelphia 76ers.

Dallas, the second-youngest team in the NBA at an average of 24.75 years old, improved to 6-4 on November 26 when Mashburn scored 50 points to power a 25-point comeback in a 124-123 overtime win at the Denver Nuggets' McNichols Arena.

The hot streak was such that in the final game of November—a home date with the Minnesota Timberwolves—the Mavs were afforded a luxury they had not enjoyed in years—winning when playing poorly. Dallas was held to 84 points and shot just 39 percent from the field but still held on for a one-point win.

The victory gave Dallas, now 7-4, its first three-game win streak since November 3-9, 1990, and its first winning month since April, 1990.

On December 6, Dallas stayed above .500 by winning its third overtime road game against a 1993-94 playoff team. This time the victim was the San Antonio Spurs in the Alamodome, 124-121, and Kidd provided one of the greatest plays of his career to make it all possible.

Dallas trailed, 112-108, with 28.4 seconds left when Mavs forward Lucious Harris connected on a three-pointer to pare the deficit to one point. San Antonio requested a timeout to settle itself, but Kidd quickly ruffled the Spurs again when he anticipated the inbounds pass along the left sideline. Kidd sprinted in front of J.R. Reid, the intended recipient of the pass, stole the ball inches from the baseline, and retained possession for the Mavs by hurtling airborne over a picket of photographers and requesting a 20-second timeout before he crashed out of bounds.

The steal, Kidd's season-high fifth of the game, made him a highlight-reel fixture, as that play was replayed endlessly all across the country. The amazing combination of quick thought (Dallas had no full one-minute timeouts left, and requesting one would have warranted a technical foul), and athleticism (holding onto the ball and touching his shoulders with his fingertips while soaring) made his uncanny effort one of the best sports plays of the year.

Kidd was not finished with the Spurs that night, however, hitting a pressure-packed jumper with 1:20 left in overtime that tied the game at 118. Jackson scored five of his 28 points in the extra session to help seal the victory.

"Jason is one of those guys you have to see every night to really appreciate," Jackson told reporters after the game. "You might see a couple of great passes on the highlights, but you won't see all the quiet, little plays he makes that helps a team win."

Kidd delivered Christmas early to both the fans of Dallas and Oakland, December 20, when he returned to his boyhood home for the first time as a professional basketball player. Kidd purchased 300 tickets for family and friends at Oakland Coliseum to make the hometowners happy, then provided some cheer for his Texas followers with 19 points, 5 rebounds, and 10 assists in a 110-107 win over the Golden State Warriors.

The victory pushed Dallas' record to 12-9, just one win shy of the previous season's final win mark, and gave the franchise its best start after 20 games since the 1988-89 season. The Mavericks appeared to have a serious shot at becoming the best single-season turnaround story in NBA history. At this early juncture of the season the Mavs possessed a shot to match the 35-win improvement the Spurs made from the 1988-89 to 89-90 seasons after it drafted David Robinson.

But most of Dallas's 12 wins had come against teams that did not make the playoffs the previous season. The make-or-break stretch of the Mavericks' schedule was rapidly approaching in the forms of the NBA's better clubs.

Dallas broke. From December 22, when the Mavericks were out-scored, 13-2, in the final 4:43 to lose, 103-101, in the Tacoma Dome to the Seattle SuperSonics, to January 31, when the Milwaukee Bucks' Vin Baker sealed a 107-105 decision by burying a last-ditch 3-pointer, Dallas' momentum came to a brake-locking halt. The Mavericks limped through that stretch at 4-17, and fell to 16-25 overall.

The Milwaukee loss was another frustrating public relations nightmare for the team, its sec-

Jason Kidd and Grant Hill each received 43 of a possible 105 votes to be named co-winners of the 1995 Rookie of the Year Award.

ond defeat on national television, and a busted showcase for Kidd. The game had been billed as the first head-to-head meeting between Robinson and Kidd, the top two picks in the previous June draft. But the Mav guard could not even make the trip after being hospitalized in Dallas with flu-like symptoms and dehydration. Kidd missed two games with the ailment before returning February 4 in a rousing 119-98 win over the Utah Jazz that broke a seven-game home losing streak.

The Mavs' horrific skid through the early parts of 1995 seemingly became unstoppable because of the bizarre new ways teams found each night to beat them. On December 27, in Dallas, the Phoenix Suns' Kevin Johnson splashed a 17-foot jump shot with 3.7 seconds left in the game for a 119-118 win. Jackson's nine-foot jumper at the buzzer rimmed out. Dallas blew a nine-point lead in the final 4:38 to lose, 116-111, at Delta Center, allowing the Utah Jazz to score on their final 12 possessions. The loss dropped the Mavs to 16-21 and ended a five-game stretch of playing teams with a .690 winning percentage.

Kidd traveled to Phoenix during the All-Star break, accepting an invitation to play in the Schick Rookie Game, an new showcase of first-year players as a warm-up for the annual All-Star Game. Kidd's luck ran as cold in the rookie affair as it had the past month with the Mavericks. He sliced to the basket for a layup that sent his Green Team into overtime with the White Team at 79-79, but his team was outscored, 4-0, in the extra session of an 83-79 defeat.

Dallas appeared rejuvenated in the second half of the season, finishing an inspiring 14-10 in its last 24 games. Maybe the team had come to accept weird defeat, maybe it had learned certain things are out of its control. But probably, the team had finally begun to fully understand itself.

Then Jim Jackson, the team's scoring leader, suffered a third-degree sprain of his left ankle that ended his season February 24 in a 114-104 loss at New Jersey. Someone would need to step up to fill the gap, and that someone was Kidd. Jason led the team in scoring four times in their last 29 games, including a 30-point effort—and a Mavs' rookie-record 17 assists—in a 130-125 win over Golden State that broke a four-game skid.

Kidd helped beat Sacramento, 91-90, the next night at the ARCO Arena with a bit of court cunning. The Kings' Mitch Richmond had apparently tied the game at 91 with a three-point shot with 4.2 seconds left, but it was ruled by officials his foot was on the line, reducing the shot to a 2-pointer. Kings surrounded the officials to argue, and the confused Mavericks, thinking the score was tied, 91-91, tried to call time out, but Kidd managed to get the inbounds pass and ran out the clock for a victory.

A week later Kidd responded to being named NBA Player of the Week for the first time by hitting 8 of 16 shots for 20 points and contributing 5 rebounds, 9 assists, 5 steals and 2 blocked shots in a 102-100 double-overtime triumph over the Cleveland Cavaliers.

Kidd, playing his best basketball of the season and powering what would eventually become a season-best six-game win streak, scored nine points in the last 4:42 and four in the final 20.6 seconds of a 117-110 upset win over Utah, which entered the game the Western Conference leader at 50-18.

Kidd's super month (he averaged 16.6 points, 4.3 rebounds, and 7.6 assists per game) did not go unnoticed as he sprung from NBA Player of the Week to NBA Rookie of the Month for March. Dallas, not coincidently, finished 10-6 in March.

Kidd kept surging and April 5 recorded his first-ever triple-double as a pro with 19 points, 10 rebounds, and 12 assists in a 130-111 upset at Reunion Arena over the red-hot Los Angeles Lakers. Kidd liked the triple-double so much he did it again two nights later in a 111-94 victory at the Minnesota Timberwolves' expense. This time Kidd netted 11 points with 10 boards and 13 assists as the resurgent Mavs won their 11th game in 14 tries.

Kidd's triple-double was the first back-to-back triple-double by a point guard since his idol, Magic Johnson, did it for the Lakers early in 1991. Remarkably, he recorded all four of his first pro season in a 10-game stretch from April 5 through April 20. No other NBA player had more than four triple-double performances that season.

Kidd put the final exclamation point on his superlative rookie season April 11 in a shocking 156-147 double-overtime win over the Houston Rockets—the team that had won the world champion the previous year and was on its way to winning a consecutive title that year.

The Rockets took a 139-128 advantage with a minute left in the first extra session, but Kidd drained three consecutive three-pointers in the next 55 seconds, the final one after he picked off a Rocket pass with 28 seconds remaining. Houston's Robert Horry hit one of two free throws on the ensuing possession for a 142-139 Rocket lead with 7.3 ticks left, but Kidd took the rebound through the defense and banged a triple-clutch, fallaway three-pointer to force a second overtime. Kidd, who hit six straight three-point tries in the fourth period and the overtimes, recorded his third triple-double in the past five games with a season-high 38 points, 11 rebounds, 10 assists, and 3 steals. His eight three-pointers (in 12 tries) set a Mavericks record, and the entire performance put Jason's name in strong contention for Rookie of the Year honors.

Dallas finished Kidd's rookie campaign 36-46, a 23-game improvement over the previous year, the sixth-best next-season comeback in NBA history. In 1993-94, Dallas's record was the worst in the NBA, but in the next year, they passed Boston, Miami, New Jersey, Philadelphia, Washington, Milwaukee, Detroit, Minnesota, and Golden State in wins.

Kidd's efforts rank him fourth all-time in rookies improving a club's win-total. List-topper David Robinson added 35 wins to the Spurs after coming aboard in 1989-90, Hall of Famer Larry Bird was plus-32 with the Celtics in 1979-80, and Hall of Famer Lew Alcindor was plus-29 with the Lakers in 1969-70.

Although Glenn Robinson had a fine year at Milwaukee, for much of the year, Grant Hill had received the bulk of the attention in the race for Rookie of the Year. Hill had not only been invited to the All-Star Game, he was the game's biggest vote getter. He averaged 19.9 points per game, plus 6.4 rebounds, and 5.0 assists. But Kidd's performances could not be overlooked, and the committee decided to award joint trophies—only the second time in NBA history that two players shared Rookie of the Year honors.

5

EXPECTATIONS

The Dallas Mavericks entered the 1995-96 season with baggage they had not carried in quite some time—expectation.

With Jackson, among the NBA scoring leaders the previous season, a healthy and happier Mashburn, and strong rebounder and bit player "Popeye" Jones a year wiser back to surround Kidd, the Mavs had been predicted by several national media outlets as a playoff team. Dallas was everyone's sleeper pick, and the Three Js seemingly had the firepower to deliver.

The season started out superbly for Kidd and the Mavericks. Kidd scored 27 points in a season-opening road win over San Antonio, then backed off his scoring as the Mavs won their home-opener over Golden State. Kidd then chipped in 15 points in a win over expansion

Seattle's Detlef Schrempf tries to guard Kidd, but Jason poured in a season-high 36 points as the Mavericks beat the SuperSonics on February 1, 1996. The Sonics went on to win the Western Conference that year.

Vancouver and 22 against Robinson and Milwaukee, and Dallas was off to a franchise-best 4-0 start. Kidd scored 25 points and grabbed 25 rebounds in a frustrating 108-102 loss to the red-hot Chicago Bulls.

The Mavericks were winning with defense, holding the Spurs, Warriors, Grizzlies, and Bucks all to less than 100 points. However, once the team's defense started to go, the Mavericks went into a heavy decline. Opponents averaged 105 points per game against Dallas in 1995-96. The Mavs reached the All-Star break with a disappointing record of 16-30.

The point guard received more than a million fan votes for the NBA All-Star Game in San Antonio. John Stockton of the Utah Jazz had handed off more assists than any other player in NBA history and Gary Payton was a real rising star. But Kidd's votes were enough for him to get the starting nod for the Western Conference. Not only was he the first Maverick to make the team since 1990, he was the first Mav ever to start the All-Star affair.

George Karl, the West head coach for the All-Star Game, said either Stockton or Payton should have started. But Kidd's statistics were outstanding. He was averaging 13.7 points, 9.0 assists, and just 3 turnovers a game at the time of the selection. He entered the game tied for fourth in the league in assists. Kidd's 6.2 rebounds a game led all point guards, and he entered the game as the NBA's only player at that point in the season with at least 700 points, 400 assists, 300 rebounds, and 100 steals. He had twice the steals of Grant Hill, more three-pointers than Anfernee Hardaway, and five more triple-doubles than Magic Johnson.

Kidd exploded into the All-Star weekend with four triple-doubles in a four-week span and achieved one of his all-time goals—a 20-assist game—when he dished out 25 in a 136-133 double-overtime upset of the Utah Jazz at Reunion Arena.

The 25-assist night was a franchise and NBA-season high. Records shattered at Kidd's side as the game progressed. He had 8 assists in the first period, 5 in the second (to break Mark Aguirre's first-half team record), 5 in the third (to tie his personal record for a game), 4 in the fourth (to break the then 1995-96 season record of Denver's Mahmoud Abdul-Rauf of 20), 1 in the first overtime, and 2 in the second.

"I set a goal of 20," Kidd said, "but I didn't think I could get it, much less 25. My teammates were feeling it, and I got them the ball. The main thing is this came in a win."

Jim Jackson "felt it" most with 38 points, and George McCloud pumped in 32. Kidd added 20 points.

Kidd said he was on "cloud nine" at the All-Star Game. He dished out a game-high 10

The Mavericks were an improved team in 1996, but they still had their problems. Here B.J. Armstrong (left) and Joe Smith combined to block Kidd's shot.

assists, scored 7 points, and grabbed 7 rebounds in just 22 minutes. Still, the East ran off with a 129-118 triumph.

Kidd used the words of Karl and Payton, who in the press decried the All-Star selections process as a "popularity contest," as a bit of personal motivation later in the season when he scored 36 points (two off his career-high) with 8 assists, 9 rebounds, and 4 steals in a 103-100 upset of the Sonics in Reunion Arena.

Kidd had taped two photocopies to his locker stall before the game, one from Karl saying, "I see John Stockton and Gary Payton as being a helluva lot better than him," and the other—Payton's remarks—for inspiration.

Great point guards aren't always the best of friends. But Jason Kidd and Gary Payton of the Seattle Super-Sonics palled around happily before the 1996 All-Star Game.

Kidd also held Payton to 20 points, 4 rebounds, and 4 assists. "He got me," Payton later admitted. "But I'll get him back. And then he'll get me back. It's great."

The Kidd-Payton matchup has grown into one of the most intense one-on-one matchups and rivalries in the NBA. Some think the duel began as just a battle between players talented in the same facets of the game playing in the same conference. In reality, it goes much deeper.

As an eighth-grader, Kidd played for a traveling all-star team coached by Payton's father. Kidd was therefore afforded some one-on-one time with Gary, who was then playing for Oregon State. The relationship grew from tutorial to competitive.

"I know his game, pretty much," Kidd said, "and that makes the rivalry fun because you have to bring something new to the floor. He knows what I can do, and I know what he can do, so that makes the rivalry fun."

Infighting, occasionally uninspired play, and injuries reduced the rest of Kidd's second year to another campaign of frustration. "We're so young," Kidd said. "Just look around this lockerroom. We made a lot of mistakes because we're all just 23, 24, 25 years old. We didn't have any of those older veterans around to stop us from doing all these silly things. It took us a while, but we now all realize how good it can be if we can just get it together and get on the same page. We can get it together. I think it can still work."

A lot of the problems that hamstrung Dallas in the 1995-96 season had nothing to do with what opponents did. Jackson, Mashburn, and Kidd were all involved in various degrees of personal bickering at some point. Jackson was still hampered by the ankle injury he suffered the year before, and a feud between him and Kidd simmered for several weeks. By now, the roller-coaster ride to the NBA lottery was unstoppable. Dallas lost eight of its next 12 after upsetting Seattle, including embarrassing back-to-back, home-and-away losses to hapless Minnesota. They also lost a home game, 121-115, to Philadelphia, the worst team in the league. A 128-112 loss to expansion Vancouver was not pretty either.

Dallas lost 10 games consecutively in March and did not come out of its dive until Kidd scored 22 points in a 117-114 upset of Houston. Kidd scored 37 points in a 123-103 loss at Phoenix in the team's next-to-last game.

The future remains bright for Kidd. In this double-overtime victory against the Utah Jazz, Kidd contributed 20 points and 25 assists despite being double teamed by Byrone Russell and Karl Malone.

Kidd ended his season with a flourish and in much the same way he began it, producing his ninth triple-double (21 points, 15 assists, 10 rebounds) of the season in a 103-98 win over the Spurs. The upset denied San Antonio a coveted 60-win season, and to a larger degree, earned the Mavs some Lone State respect and bragging rights.

Kidd finished the 1995-96 season second behind only sure-bet Hall of Famer Stockton in assists, with 9.7 per game. He was fourth in the league with 2.16 steals per game. Kidd was 36th in the league in scoring (16.6), and led all NBA guards with 6.8 rebounds per game.

Kidd improved in every statistical category except shooting percentage. His personal production was better than his rookie year, but his second NBA season ended as another disappointment. As Hill and the Detroit Pistons prepared for the Eastern Conference playoffs, he and the Mavs were left to ponder another lost season and whom Dallas would select with another lottery pick.

Dallas finished 26-56, 10 losses worse than the 1994-95 campaign that had given many in Dallas big hopes. The Mavs finished ahead of only expansion Vancouver (15-67) in the Western Conference and with the fifth-worst record in the league (tied with Minnesota).

Kidd lobbied hard at season's end for the team to upgrade its center position, the spot on the team in greatest need of revamping. Money could prove to be no object in the Mavericks future as the franchise was bought in late April by a group headed by Texas billionaire and political aspirant H. Ross Perot.

But the Mavericks' poor season was not the only basketball disappointment of 1996. Kidd's dream of playing for the United States "Dream Team" in the 1996 Summer Olympics in Atlanta was dashed when he was passed over in selection for the team. Grant Hill and Glenn Robinson, however, were chosen. Robinson, though withdrew because of an injury. His spot was then awarded to Gary Payton.

Ironically, and disappointingly for Kidd, two of the top three players in his rookie draft were chosen, and he was the exception. Kidd considered himself a long-shot despite serious lobbying for him by Hill, Stockton, and David Robinson. He said he would have filled the final spots with himself and Shawn Kemp if the choice were his. But, in statements made at the All-Star Game, he seemed resigned to get ready for Dream Team IV and the 2000 Olympics.

"I'm still young," Jason said, "so if not this year then next time for sure."

With the Mavs off to another poor start in 1996, new coach Jim Cleamons made a stunning trade on the day after Christmas. He shipped Kidd off to Phoenix. Before the season was over, he also traded Jamal Mashburn and Jimmy Jackson—the three J's who were supposed to bring the good times to Dallas. With the Suns, Kidd found himself on a team that already was rich in point guards and Jason could only guess whether he might be soon be traded again.

Jason Kidd is a work in progress. He has seen and accomplished much in his two-plus decades, but clearly has more to give, as both a player and person. As his high school coach, Frank Laporte says, "He can't stand losing. He won't let that happen too long."

But basketball isn't the only thing in his life. He's a father, a husband-to-be, a lover of Chinese food, Robert DeNiro movies, R&B music, and owner of a monster of a Rottweiler named Mia, who was a gift from Seattle Seahawks lineman Sam Adams.

Kidd continues to matter off the court as well as on, however, as the hordes of children in the Kidd's Kids section, or at countless school assemblies he attends can attest.

As a real-life hero his fans can see and touch, Kidd has proven that dreams can come true if talent is polished with hard work. Hard times can be overcome if discipline and good judgment win out over impetuousness and recklessness. Someday the slinky moves, the cross-court passes, the sticky defense will not be there, but he seems determined to make sure a good person is there when the athlete is gone.

For now, though, he continues to create substance on the basketball floor where there was before only possibility, striving toward that Magic Johnson-ness that inspired him when he was a little kid parked in front of the television.

Perhaps because he knows out there, somewhere, right now, there's somebody on an asphalt court who wants to grow up and be just like Jason Kidd.

STATISTICS

JASON KIDD

University of California

Year	G	FGM	FGA	PCT	FTM	FTA	PCT	REB	AST	ST	PTS	AVG
1992-93	29	133	287	.463	88	134	.657	142	222	110	378	13.0
1993-94	30	166	352	.472	117	169	.692	207	272	94	500	16.7
TOTALS	59	299	639	.468	205	303	.677	349	494	204	878	14.9

Dallas Mavericks

Year	G	FGM	FGA	PCT	FTM	FTA	PCT	REB	AST	ST	PTS	AVG
1994-95	79	330	857	.385	192	275	.698	430	607	151	922	11.7
1995-96	81	493	1293	.381	229	331	.692	553	783	175	1348	16.6
TOTALS	160	823	2150	.383	421	606	.695	983	1390	326	2270	14.2

G	game
FGA	field goals attempted
FGM	field goals made
PCT	percent
FTA	free throws attempted
FTM	free throws made
REB	rebounds
AST	assists
PTS	points
AVG	scoring average

JASON KIDD:
A CHRONOLOGY

1973   Jason Kidd born on March 23

1991   Leads St. Joseph to a state championship.

1992   Leads St. Joseph to a second state championship; enrolls at the
       University of California.

1993   Golden Bears make only their second appearance in the NCAA
       tournament in 33 years. Kidd bursts onto the national scene by helping
       upset two-time defending championship team, Duke University.

1994   Golden Bears again invited to the NCAA tournament but are upset by
       Wisconsin-Green Bay. Kidd announces he is leaving college early to
       make himself available to the NBA draft. Despite damaging his
       reputation by leaving the scene of a car accident and fathering a child
       out of wedlock, Kidd is picked number two in the draft by the Dallas
       Mavericks.

1995   Kidd is chosen co-Rookie of the Year (with Grant Hill). Mavericks win 23
       more games than previous year, although they are still not a playoff-
       caliber team.

1996   Kidd becomes the first Maverick ever to start at the All-Star Game.

1997   Kidd is traded to the Phoenix Suns.

SUGGESTIONS FOR FURTHER READING

Hoffer, Richard, "New Kids on the Block," *Sports Illustrated,* November 23, 1992.

Taylor, Phil, "Inside College Basketball," *Sports Illustrated,* December 14, 1992.

Wolff, Alexander, "Changing of the Guard," *Sports Illustrated,* March 29, 1993.

ABOUT THE AUTHOR

Brant James is a sports reporter based on the eastern shore of Maryland. A graduate of West Virginia University, James has covered Major League baseball and the NBA plus major college athletics in different roles from beat writer to sports editor.

INDEX